ON THE MOUND

. . . .

ıst concentrate, I thought.

I put my foot on the rubber.

I checked the runners.

And the storm broke.

The runners started screaming: "Look at me, Tip. ey, Tip, I'm going. I'm going . . ."

Their third and first base coaches were shouting o. "O'Hara'll blow, Gus. He's got rabbit ears. He's stening to me right now."

In the stands their parents were calling out: "Let ip walk you, Gus. He can't pitch . . ."

Joe was screaming at me: "Don't listen to them, ip. Pitch to me."

I nodded. Looked back once more at the dancing, ıunting runners. I tried to empty my mind of everyıing but the fact that I had in my right hand a ball ıd I had to throw that ball over the plate to Joe awkins.

I whirled and fired home. I missed the outside corer just by inches.

"Ball one," the ump shouted.

Rabbit Ears

Rabbit Ears

by Alfred Slote

HarperTrophy

A Division of HarperCollinsPublishers

Rabbit Ears
Copyright © 1982 by Alfred Slote
All rights reserved. Printed in the United States of America.
No part of this book may be used or reproduced in any manner whatsoever
without written permission except in the case of brief quotations embodied
in critical articles and reviews. For information address HarperCollins
Children's Books, a division of HarperCollins Publishers,
10 East 53rd Street, New York, NY 10022

Library of Congress Cataloging-in-Publication Data
Slote, Alfred.
  Rabbit ears.

  Summary: In order to become a good pitcher for his baseball team, fifteen-
year-old Tip tries to overcome his sensitivity to the jeers of the opposing players.
  [1. Baseball—Fiction]   I. Title.
PZ7.S635Rab   1982   [Fic]   81-47760
ISBN 0-397-31988-6   AACR2
ISBN 0-397-31989-4 (lib. bdg.)
ISBN 0-06-440134-0 (pbk.)
First Harper Trophy edition, 1983.

For Elizabeth

Contents

1

Pitching Change

We were playing United Uniform. We were leading 3–2 in the top of the seventh when Vince Mendoza, our pitcher, walked the first two guys.

"Time, ump," Mr. Corunna, our coach, called, and trotted out to the mound.

Out in left field, my heart started to pound. He was going to call on me to pitch. I just knew it was coming. Marty Regan, our other starting pitcher, had gone up north with his folks for a vacation. That left me as the only other pitcher.

Don't call on me, I prayed. Ask someone else.

But I could see Mr. Corunna glancing at me as he talked to Vince. Joe Dawkins, our catcher, was also looking my way.

"You gonna be it, man," Willie Thomas, our center fielder, called over to me.

"Thanks a lot," I yelled back.

"You can do the job, Tip," Willie said. "You got the arm. Just close them big ears of yours."

Willie meant well. But that hurt. I had rabbit ears. The biggest rabbit ears in the Arborville fifteen-year-old league. Everyone knew that you could get Tip O'Hara to blow his cool by yelling at him. Dad said I had the O'Hara Irish temper. Mom said I simply was too sensitive.

Whatever the reason, because of my rabbit ears I'd gone from being a really good pitcher to just an ordinary left fielder. But I liked it out here in left field. It was peaceful and quiet.

I wanted to stay out here.

"OK, Tip," Mr. Corunna called out, "come on in. You're pitching."

Vince was trotting out to left field. We were to trade places. Vince was a good hitter. You couldn't keep him out of the lineup.

Our paths crossed around shortstop.

Vince grinned at me. "Save the win for me, Tip."

"I'll do my best, man."

"Don't pay no attention if they start mouthing off."

"Righto. I'll just shut them out."

That was a pun. A joke. But neither of us laughed.

The infield was gathered around the pitcher's mound. George Kosmowski, our big first baseman; Bobby Bell, our second baseman; Chico Morales, our shortstop; and Ed Tinker, our third baseman. Joe Dawkins, only the best catcher in Arborville, was looking at me grimly through the bars of his mask. He knew what I was going through.

Mr. Corunna handed me the ball.

"Well, Tip," he said, "this is it. A new season. You think you can ignore them?"

An honest answer was no. But you never give honest answers to coaches. If you've got double pneumonia and a broken leg and a coach asks you how you feel, you're supposed to say "great." Coaches know you're lying anyway, so what difference does it make?

"Sure," I said. "I won't hear a word they say."

"Thata boy," Mr. Corunna said, and he slapped me on the back.

"Mow 'em down, baby," Chico said.

"You're my man," Ed Tinker said, and slapped me on the rear end with his glove.

Kosmowski grunted. Bobby Bell winked at me. It's funny. The left side of our infield, Chico and Ed—they talk a lot. The right side is quiet. Sometime I'll figure that one out.

Everyone went back to their positions except Joe. He's my best friend on the team.

"Listen, Tip," he said, "when they start yelling, you just look twice as hard at me. Right?"

"Right."

"And you try to hear what *I'm* saying, cause *I'm* gonna be talking to you all the time."

"Gotcha."

"One finger's fast and two's off-speed, and that's all we're gonna go with. You watch where I set my target. And pitch to it. Remember, these guys are humpty-dumpties. They finished next to last last year, and they're gonna finish last this year. Forget about the runners on base. We work the batter. OK?"

"OK."

I could hardly hear Joe, my heart was pounding so. I glanced over at their bench. They were grinning already, waiting for the right moment. They remembered last year. Everyone remembered how I'd blown last year. How the word got around that I had rabbit ears. One team finds it out, and pretty soon the whole league knows it.

Their coaches on the bases were grinning and so were their base runners. They had two girls on their team, and they were grinning too.

It was going to happen again. I could feel it. It was in the air. I looked around.

"For Pete's sake," Joe said, "don't look around. If you don't see, you won't hear."

"Right," I said.

But that wasn't true. And we both knew it.

2
Noise on the Diamond

They were quiet while I took my warm-up pitches. But that would be part of their plan. They'd hit me with the noise all at once.

Meanwhile, around me, my team—Acme Lumber—was talking it up loudly:

"Lookin' good, Tip."

"They can't hit, Tip."

"Easy on, easy off, Tipper man."

I wasn't sure what that last one meant, but it sounded good.

I could even hear my outfielders. Hilda Sims

out in right field chanting over and over: "Nothing to worry about, Tip. Nothing to worry about, Tip."

She sounded like *she* was worried.

In center field, Willie Thomas in a high squeaky voice: "You're my man, Tip. You're my man."

And in left field, Vince Mendoza, who wanted a win in the first game of the season, was yelling: "Give'em smoke, Tip. They can't see smoke."

I had a good fastball. It moved on batters. In the twelve- and thirteen-year-old leagues, I was one of the best pitchers in the league. Then last year in the fourteen-year-old league, they discovered I had rabbit ears. That I could be rattled.

"One more, Tip," Dave Kosko, the ump called out. He's a pretty good ump. He's seventeen and umped in our league last year. The umps move up with the kids.

I laid some smoke right over the heart of the plate. Joe made a little approving fist at me and fired the ball back. I wished Mr. Corunna would ask Joe to pitch sometime. He fires that ball back to a pitcher as hard as a pitcher fires to him. But he's the only guy on our team who can play catcher.

I kicked some dirt around the mound while

the United Uniform batter came up to the plate. It was a guy named Gus Contakos. A big, fattish kind of kid.

A big target.

Just concentrate, I thought.

I put my foot on the rubber.

I checked the runners.

And the storm broke.

The runners started screaming: "Look at me, Tip. Hey, Tip, I'm going. I'm going . . ."

Their third base and first base coaches were shouting too. By the rules of the Arborville Recreation Baseball Leagues, the base coaches (almost always adults) are not allowed to yell at the pitcher. But these fathers got around it by pretending they were yelling at their batter.

"O'Hara'll blow, Gus. He's got rabbit ears. He's listening to me right now."

I was.

And in the stands their parents were calling out: "Let Tip walk you, Gus. He can't pitch . . ."

Joe was screaming at me: "Don't listen to them, Tip. Pitch to me."

And now their bench finally joined the chorus. "Hey, pitcherpitcher . . ."

"Hey, Tippytiptip . . ."

"Look out behind you, Tip."

"Hoo, hoo, O'Hara."

"Tip," Joe yelled desperately, "throw the ball!"

I nodded. Looked back once more at the dancing, taunting runners. I tried to empty my mind of everything but the fact that I had in my right hand a ball and I had to throw that ball over the plate to Joe Dawkins.

I whirled and fired home. I missed the outside corner just by inches.

"Ball one," Kosko shouted.

Joe turned and squawked. He was squawking for my sake. Letting me know he thought that pitch was good enough for a strike.

It wasn't, but it should have been good enough to shut up the United Uniform team.

It didn't.

"He's wild, Gus."

"Let him walk you, Gus."

"Tip's up, up, up . . ."

"Good chuck, Tip," Mr. Corunna yelled over the noise.

And behind me my team was also shouting.

There was so much noise. I felt like I was drowning in it. I wanted to close my eyes and swim to shore.

I went to a stretch position. The runners led off, yelling and waving their hands.

Nuts to you, I thought.

I fired. Way wide this time.

Their bench cheered.

Joe came out halfway with the ball.

"Just hit my target, Tip. It's as easy as walking, man."

I nodded. But it wasn't true. Walking is easier than pitching. When you go for a walk, no one's screaming at you "hey, walkerwalkerwalker," or "walker's going up, up, up" or "walker, your socks smell."

I wished I were walking home right now.

My third pitch bounced in the dirt four feet in front of the plate. Joe tried to block it with his body. But it got by him. I forgot to cover home. I just stared at everyone running, listened to everyone screaming. The runner from second scored. The guy on first went to third. And Mr. Corunna called time.

"Goodbye, O'Hara," someone on their team yelled.

"Short season, Tip."

Mr. Corunna's face was grim. Joe came out from behind the plate. Chico from short. They didn't allow more than two players plus a coach.

"Tip," Mr. Corunna said softly, "we'll get that run back. But let's not give them the game, son."

"Yes, sir."

"If they're going to win, make them beat us. Let's not beat ourselves. Get the ball over, Tip. Let them hit it, if they can. They can't. That's why they're yelling so much. Contakos can't hit you."

That's what Mr. Corunna said to me, and he was right. Contakos couldn't hit me. One reason was that on my next pitch to him, I hit him. Right on his left hip.

United Uniform went wild with glee.

"He's gonna kill us."

"He's wild, wild, wild."

"Give'm a hunting license, ump."

Contakos wasn't hurt. He was very happy to get a free ride to first base.

Joe came out from behind the plate. He looked angry. Chico came in from shortstop.

"They're stalling, ump. Don't let'em stall."

"Oh, shut up," I yelled at them.

"For Pete's sake, Tip," Joe said, "don't talk to them."

"Stop listening to them, Tip," Chico said.

"I'm trying not to."

"Just play catch with me," Joe said.

Easier said than done.

The ump came out and told us to get on with the game.

The next United Uniform batter was a little wiry kid named Glen Withersbee, who always spit a lot. As if he were a tough kid.

Joe gave me two fingers for an off-speed. We weren't going to try to blow it by Withersbee. We were just going to let the punk hit it.

As I got set to pitch, I heard the following things:

"How's the rabbit ears today, Tip?"

"Can you get Channel 4 on your rabbit ears, Tip?"

"I bet you eat a lot of carrots when you're not pitching, O'Hara."

"Ball one," Kosko said, as the pitch went behind Withersbee, and Joe made a great diving catch.

"O'Hara, you're supposed to throw in front of him."

"You trying to hit him in the butt, Tip?"

"Better put your helmet on your fanny, Glen."

That was so stupid I wanted to shout back: Can't you bench jockeys think of anything clever to shout?

My next pitch was wide the other way.

"Ball two," Kosko said.

"Come on, Tip," Mr. Corunna called out, and I could tell he was giving up on me.

"Pitch to me, Tip," Joe yelled angrily.

"He would if he could, Joe."

"He can't see you, Joe."

"Better get him a Seeing Eye dog."

"Ball three," Kosko said, as I was way up with a pitch.

"Tip's up, up, up," they chanted.

"He's pitched you in every direction except down," the first base coach yelled.

Everyone laughed.

At 3 and 0 I decided to go to a full windup. Contakos was slow. He wouldn't run. As I started my windup, someone on their bench yelled:

"Hey, Tip, your laces are untied."

The oldest gag in the world. The stupidest gag in the world.

I'll never know why I did it, but I did. Right

in the middle of my windup, I broke my motion and looked down at my shoelaces.

"That's a balk," Kosko yelled. "Base runners advance."

The runner from third trotted in, and Contakos trotted over to second.

And with that, Mr. Corunna had enough.

3

Harsh Words

We lost 7–5. I let in two runs and then Chico, who can't really pitch, gave up a whole bunch of hits, and we lost the first game of the season to a lousy team like United Uniform.

They were all grins and making snide comments when they came over to shake hands.

One of them said, "Tough luck, Tip."

They tried to keep their faces straight when they shook hands with me, but right after they'd be grinning. They'd stolen a game and they knew it.

Joe Dawkins glared after them. "We're gonna beat the daylight out of them next time. They're a bunch of creeps."

No one spoke to me. I was glad of that at least. We headed for the parking lot. Parents were standing there, leaning against cars, the men talking to men, mothers to mothers. They didn't seem particularly unhappy about our loss. It's a kind of social thing for parents when it's over.

I was glad my folks don't come to baseball games.

My bike was chain-locked to a tree. I had got it unlocked when I realized Mr. Corunna was shouting at us.

"Where're you people going?" he yelled. "I didn't say you could go home. I want everyone back on the bench."

"Oh, boy," I heard Chico say, "now we're gonna catch it."

"We deserve it," Joe said.

Ed Tinker shook his head. "This is one game best forgot, I say."

"Duvall," Mr. Corunna snapped, "get the equipment into the bag."

Eddie Duvall is a sub infielder. No one knows why he sticks with the team year after year. All he gets to do is pack and carry the equipment bag. I felt sorry for him. I got up to help him.

"Sit down, Tip," Mr. Corunna said. "This time I *want* you listening."

That drew a few snickers. I sat down feeling my face aflame. Don Corunna, another sub, the coach's son, got up to help Duvall.

Off in the parking lot, the United Uniform kids could be heard congratulating one another on a "good game." They acted as though they had really beat us. We played them again next Monday. It would be a different story then.

"Regan'll be back," George Kosmowski growled. "We'll eat those creeps up next Monday."

The other guys just spat or kicked the dirt.

"All right," Mr. Corunna said, "I'll make this short but not too sweet. Today was a mess. We handed them the game. Player for player we're better than they are at every position. But we made them a gift. Thursday night we have a night game at Vets against Belden Hardware. They're a good team. If we lose to a team like United Uniform, what's going to happen when we play Belden?"

"Regan'll be back, won't he, Coach?" Stan Bacon, a sub, asked.

"Regan won't be back till Sunday," Mr. Corunna said.

Everyone groaned. Me too.

"The fact is we can't count on any single player to save us. We have to save ourselves. And we can. We've got the ball players. They're right here on this bench, right now."

I felt a couple of the guys sneaking doubtful looks at me.

"And don't look at Tip either," Mr. Corunna went on. "He had his problems today, but we're going to work on those problems. We're going to help Tip lick his problems. All right, that's it for now. But I want to have a special practice tomorrow over at Sampson Park."

We didn't usually practice once the season started. There were two games a week. That was usually enough. We'd been practicing every other day for a month now.

"There're games at Sampson, Mr. Corunna."

"Not at one o'clock."

More groans. It was hot in Arborville at one on summer afternoons.

"Quit that," Mr. Corunna snapped. "If we

don't straighten out right now, it's going to be a long season. Who *can't* make it?"

"I can't," Chico said.

"Why not?"

"I've got to help my dad every day."

Chico's dad ran a lawn service.

"I'll call your father tonight," Mr. Corunna said. "Who else?"

Duvall raised his hand. He was trying to stuff a bat into the already jammed equipment bag. "I'm in a swim meet tomorrow."

"You're excused," Mr. Corunna said.

"What's your stroke, Eddie?" Chico asked.

Eddie turned red. I felt sorry for him. Not as sorry as I felt for myself, but sorry enough.

"Willie?"

"I'll be there."

"Hilda?"

"I can make it," Hilda said. She never missed a practice. She was a good fielder, but she was weak on hitting. Mr. Corunna always gave her more hitting practice than the others.

"Joe?"

"Yeah."

"George?"

"I'll be there . . ."

He'd asked who couldn't be there. Why was he now singling out people and asking them if they could be there? I knew why. He wanted to make doubly certain I'd be there, but he didn't want to single me out.

"Tip?"

"Yes, sir," I said quietly.

"Good. One o'clock, Diamond Two, Sampson Park. I'll see you boys tomorrow. Those of you going to the Sampson Park parking lot in my truck, get over there now. I'll be right along. Tip, I want to talk alone with you for a moment."

I knew it was coming. He wouldn't be a coach if he didn't talk with me alone. I had lost the game. Not Joe or Chico or Bell or George . . .

He waited till everyone had left. He was decent about that. I had to hand him that. A tough coach, but he thought about your feelings.

We watched Duvall and Don carry the equipment bag over to the truck and then heave it over the side. On the side of the truck it said MATTRESSES. Mr. Corunna managed a mattress factory. I guess business wasn't so good. He seemed to be able to take off any time of the day to coach us.

The last of the Acme Lumbers had moved off.

Mr. Corunna sat down on the bench alongside me.

"OK, Tip, what about it?"

"I'm sorry."

"Sorry won't help."

I didn't know what else to say.

"It's all in your head, you know that."

"Yes, sir."

"What are you going to do about it?"

"I don't know."

He was silent a moment. "Tip, answer me honestly. Do you like playing baseball?"

"Yes, I do," I said honestly.

"Then why can't you shut out the noise?"

"I don't know."

He gazed at me for a moment. "Do you want to be able to?"

"More than anything in the world, coach."

He was coming to a decision.

"All right, then, tomorrow we're going to meet your problem head on. Tomorrow I'm going to work *with* you and *on* you. I'm going to give you a harder time than any opposing team ever gave you. And I'm going to have your teammates give you a hard time. It's not going to be personal, Tip, but it will probably sound like it."

"Yes, sir. I understand."

"I don't know if you do. Tip, riding a pitcher, bench jockeying, is something that happens in the big leagues. We don't allow it, as you know, in the nine-, ten-, eleven-, and twelve-year-old leagues. No one's allowed to yell at the pitcher by name. I'm not sure whether that rule's good or bad. But while the league office doesn't approve of it in the thirteen-and-up leagues, we let it happen. You know why we let it happen."

I knew why, but he wanted me to say no, so I said, "No, sir."

"Because it's part of life. It's a part of baseball as it's played on the highest levels, and baseball is a part of life. You learn to play and you learn to live through taunts, jeers, bench jockeying. You'll be the better man for it. Do you understand?"

He was taking a long time to say what Dad said last year when I complained about kids yelling at me: "If you can't stand the heat, get out of the kitchen," he had said.

"All right, then, Tip, let me just add this. We need you this season. We'll need you even after Regan gets back. No team can last a season with only two pitchers. You're our third pitcher, and by God, you are a pitcher, Tip. You've got the arm—what we can't give you, what you were born with. What you don't have yet is a tough head. And that's what I'm going to try to give you. Starting tomorrow. Are you willing to work with me?"

"Yes, sir."

"Good." He slapped me on the back. "Now go home and don't think anything more about it. Tomorrow's another day. Right?"

"Right."

He walked to his truck. I walked to my bike. I was very glad to get out of there.

4

Noise in the Basement

The game against United Uniform had been at West Park. The shortest way home from West Park to our house is up Huron, Washtenaw, and then down Ferdon.

But that might be getting home too fast. The clock on the Arco station at Miller and Spring said it was 7:15. Mom and Dad would still be at the dinner table. My kid brother, Roland, would be there too. Then would come the questions . . .

If I took my time going home, if I went by

way of side streets across town and then up Packard and Granger . . . by then Mom would be
upstairs at her desk, catching up on paperwork,
or outside gardening—and Dad, with luck, would
be asleep on the couch.

Dad's an engineer for the highway department.
He says he likes to catnap. He's recharging batter-
ies. Mom says, "You're not recharging, you're
snoring."

I took my time getting home. Biking up one
street and down another past a lot of little houses
with kids playing in front, squirting garden hoses
at each other. Folks sitting on porches, older kids
washing down their cars . . .

I must have passed a couple of hundred people
and not one of them knew me or knew what a
fool I'd made of myself on the diamond.

I waited for a green light at the corner of Main
and Madison. A pickup truck filled with ball players—an eleven-year-old team, it looked like—was
also stopped at the light. The kids looked down
from the truck at me; my uniform, my spikes
and glove hanging from my handlebars.

"You win?" one of the little kids asked me.

I shook my head.

"We did," he said.

"12–1," another little kid said.

"What's the name of your team?" the first kid asked me.

"Acme Lumber," I said, looking up at the red light. Come on, change!

"We're Miller Appliance," a couple of them said. "And we won."

They banged their bats on the sides of the truck. A coach sitting in front looked out the window at me and grinned.

And then, finally, the light changed.

I biked up Madison, down Fifth, up Hoover, down State, and then turned left and went up Dewey, White, and finally over to Packard and up to Granger.

I was really taking my time. By the time I hit Granger and Baldwin, just a couple of blocks from my house, I had almost put the nightmare of our ball game out of my mind. I'd get some soda pop and watch TV. Tomorrow morning I'd mow Mrs. Gardner's lawn and clip Mrs. Kappler's bushes. After baseball practice, I'd go fishing down at the river. The fishing would be a reward for the baseball. I loved fishing and I loved the river. No one hollered at you when you fished; the riverbank was always quiet.

By the time I hit the corner of Granger and Ferdon, only about sixty feet (or the distance from the pitcher's mound to home plate) from where we lived, I was feeling a lot better.

It didn't last.

I heard our house before I saw it.

The noise came blasting out of our basement windows. It was unbelievable.

"Hello, hello," Roland shouted into a microphone.

And two other voices shouted back:

"Hellodeedododo . . ."

And then the music started, and the singing (if you could call it that).

Hellodeedododo
Hellodeedododo
You can hello it all day long
You can sing it or sway it
As long as you play it
You can make yourself a song
Songdeedongdongdong
Songdeedongdongdong . . .

I knew what it was, of course. My brother, Roland, is a musician. He's only eleven years old and in sixth grade, but he and a pal of his named Paul Wings have a rock band. They make a lot of crazy noise, just the two of them.

Roland's always after me to play in the band. I taught him to play the guitar, and I sing. Except for Dad, our whole family is musical. Mom plays the piano and sings in the church choir. Her parents were both musicians. Music runs in the family, but it never ran this loudly, or this crazily.

I heard a girl call out:

"Give us another one, Roland."

"No, you do one, Peggy."

Good grief. Had Peggy Anderson joined Roland's baby band? Peggy was going into ninth grade like me. She lived up the block.

"Shoefly," she said into the microphone. Their amplified laughter came through the windows.

And then they started singing:

Shoeflydeedyedyedye
Shoeflydeedyedyedye
You can shoefly it all day long
You can sing it or sway it
As long as you play it
You can make yourself a song

Songdeedongdongdong
Songdeedongdongdong

It was gibberish and it was noise. And it was just about the last thing I needed right now.

I slammed my bike against Roland's in the garage and stomped in the back door. Their noise came blasting up the stairwell.

"Shut up down there!" I hollered.

This was their answer.

"Love!"

Lovedeedovedovedove
Lovedeedovedovedove
You can love it all day long
You can sing it or sway it
As long as you play it
You can make yourself a song . . .

Peggy Anderson was singing louder than the two kids. Had she completely flipped?

I'd stop them right now.

I flicked the light switch at the top of the stairs to warn them.

They went right on:

Songdeedongdongdong
Songdeedongdongdong

Had the world gone crazy? First on the baseball field. Now in my own house. Was everyone out to get me?

I went down into the basement and looked around.

Roland was playing lead guitar. Paul Wings, a shrimpy kid, was playing bass. And Peg Anderson was belting out with the biggest voice in town.

"Cut it out!" I yelled at them.

They didn't hear me. I could have dropped a bomb and they wouldn't have heard it. They had their amps turned way up.

Well, there was only one way to shut them up and I took it. I walked right through the middle of their little lunatic band and pulled one plug after another. First Roland's guitar, the amps, then Peggy's microphone.

And finally there was silence.

"What did you do that for?" Roland asked.

His lips were quivering with shock. He's a fat, little sensitive kid. He drives me nuts. Just looking at him drives me nuts. No less listening to him.

"You're making too much noise."

"It's not noise, Tip. It's music. We're working

on a new kind of song. The audience is supposed to—"

"Wait a second, Roland," Peggy Anderson cut in. "We don't owe him any explanations. He owes us one. This is your house too, isn't it?"

"That's right," Roland said. "Mom and Dad said we could rehearse here tonight, Tip. We've been invited to be in a Battle of the Bands Saturday at Sampson Park. We were going to ask you to play with us Saturday. We need a rhythm guitar and someone to sing along with Peggy."

"I've got a lot better things to do, thanks."

"Boy, you really are a grump, aren't you?" Peggy said to me.

Roland looked at me curiously. "How did your ball game go, Tip?"

"That's got nothing to do with anything."

"You lost. Did you pitch, Tip? Did they holler at you?"

I felt my face turning red. "You're asking for a poke in the nose, you know that, don't you?"

"Aw, Tip," Roland said. "You got musician's ears. Not baseball ears. Come and sit in with us."

He started plugging in the amps and the mike.

Peggy and Wings looked at me without expression.

"Come on, Tip," Roland said. "We're not going to win without a rhythm guitar and another vocalist."

"You're not going to win, period. Keep it down."

As I hit the top step I heard Roland call out: "Tip's a grump. Grump!"

Peggy and Wings sang back:

Grumpdeedumpdumpdump
Grumpdeedumpdumpdump
You can grump it all day long
You can sing it or sway it
As long as you play it
You can make yourself a song
Songdeedongdongdong
Songdeedongdongdong

"Go to hell, all of you!" I shouted down the basement stairs.

But, of course, they couldn't hear me.

I went back into the garage and got my bike. I had to find someplace quiet. There was only one place I knew that was always quiet.

I went there.

5

Down at the River

I biked down Geddes and bumped across the Amtrack tracks and turned left to the wild part of the riverbank—where the ducks gather and the fish swim.

I wasn't going down to the river to fish. I was going to the only place in Arborville where a guy can hear himself think.

I love the river.

You can be a freak and the river will ignore you. You can be stupid and miserable, happy and carefree—it doesn't make any difference to the river.

I laid down my bike in the tall grass and waded through the weeds down to the riverbank. It was dark, but I could see the big, flat rock that juts out over the water. It's one of my favorite fishing spots.

I sat down on it and looked at the water running by. It took me a few minutes before my eyes got used to the darkness, but after that I began to see things. Like the old tree that had fallen into the river years ago and made a good spot for fish to nest. I saw some brush drifting along with the current, looking like an old Spanish sailing ship (whatever they look like). And then out in the middle of the stream I caught sight of something else drifting. It was a rowboat at a loose anchor. And two men were fishing from it.

I could hear them talk in low voices. And then, every once in a while, the man at the stern would jerk back his arm and cast out. There was that lovely *fsss* sound as his line unreeled . . . and then the soft gentle *plop* of his lure hitting the surface of the water.

And then the slow reeling in.

Fishing at night is fun. You see a lot of stars.

Dad and I have fished at night a few times here in town, but generally he's too tired after work to go fishing. But when we go up north on vacations, we'll fish night and day. Fishing's serious stuff with me and Dad. Roland doesn't like fishing. There's not enough action for him. But I love it. Almost as much as I love baseball.

Things are happening in baseball when you don't think they're happening. Like what's the guy gonna throw next, and will he steal on this guy's slow curve, and you got him out on a high pitch before, does he remember? (Sure he does.)

Fishing's like that too. It's all happening below the surface, and you got to have the skills and the patience.

I sure had it for fishing.

The river was moving fast for summer. Every once in a while I could hear a fish jump somewhere, as fish will on hot nights, looking for bugs. The two fishermen in the rowboat would hear it too, and they'd talk quietly. You always want to go where the fish are feeding, but fishing is really getting them to come to you. You can chase fish down to Lake Erie and never catch a one.

It was quiet, all right. The only noise was an occasional car on Geddes Road, and an airplane, landing lights on, beginning its descent to Detroit's Metro airport forty miles away.

Give me a river anytime for peace. Even when there are people around fishing, it's quiet. Oh, if you get a bite they might pop over to see what kind of bait you're using. And if you catch a fish, they'll come over and congratulate you. Everyone wishes you well in fishing. Which is just the opposite of baseball.

Darn baseball. You love it and you can't take it. What are you going to do about it, Tip O'Hara? About your rabbit ears?

I sat there and tried to think my way through it. Figure it out.

Maybe having rabbit ears in baseball is just as bad as having only one arm or one leg. You wouldn't dream of playing baseball if you only had one arm or one leg. Of course, there are kids like that who do play ball. You read about them in the newspaper or see them on TV. But they're exceptions. They're really tough, determined kids. I was just a normal kid who had two big handicaps sticking out from either side of his head.

Maybe rabbit ears is an incurable disease, and you ought to quit the team, O'Hara.

But I love playing, I answered myself. It's just *listening* that wrecks me.

Then maybe the trick is *not* to get rid of your rabbit ears, O'Hara, but to develop a thick skin, so that insults bounce off it like bugs off a screen.

OK. How do I go about developing a thick skin, especially when I seem to have a thin one?

I lay there on that rock over the river and found no answers inside my head. I lay there and watched the water move below me and found no answers down there either.

And then . . . I saw something. I leaned forward.

I peered down.

Something more than the current was moving down there. Something big and black, and it wasn't a piece of driftwood, because it was swimming. It was a fish. A big fish. And he was just inches away from me.

I stared at it. It was a gigantic carp moseying around the underside of my rock, looking for things to nibble on.

I couldn't believe it. Of all times to be next to a big fish and me with no rod, no net, nothing . . . nothing but my two hands.

I hesitated for just a second.

Two hands it would have to be.

I inched even closer to the surface of the water. This guy was the granddaddy of all carp in the Huron River, and he had no idea I was so close to him.

I had to move fast . . . and sure.

One, I counted silently . . .

Two . . .

Three!

I shot my right hand down through the surface of the water, and my arm and shoulder and then all of me was falling into the water, but I had him! I had the fish! In one hand, and then in both my hands, and then swoosh, he shot out through my fingers like a torpedo and was gone with a gigantic splash. I stood there, all wet, soaked, standing there in three feet of water with nothing to show for it but fish smell on my hands.

I started to laugh.

I mean, what else could I do?

I was laughing really hard.

One of the men in the boat called out to me, "You all right over there?"

"Yes, sir," I gasped. I was still laughing so hard I almost lost my balance and went under again.

"Well, then," the fisherman said, "try to be quiet. We're fishing over here and fishin's a serious business."

"Yes, sir," I said. And thought: It sure can be a funny business too.

Then, as quietly as I could, I hauled myself out of the water and crawled up into the grass. I shook myself out like an old dog. I took off my shirt and wrung it out and then tied it to the handlebars of my bike. Then I took my shoes off and let the river spill out of them. I tied them together by the laces and looped them over the handlebars too. My socks were soaked. So I removed them and also tied them to the handlebars.

Then I biked home. I was glad it was dark and no one could see me. I must have looked like a crazy sight on my bike.

It took me forever to get home. It was uphill, and my pants were so wet I squeaked when I pedaled.

I could hear myself; *I* was noisy.

I started laughing all over again. I was still laughing when I put my bike away in the garage.

My laughter stopped, though, when I got to the front door.

6

Apologies Are in Order

"He's got to get out of baseball. It's making him a nervous wreck."

Dad was talking. And I was listening. Standing on the front steps, soaking wet, listening once again to things I shouldn't be hearing. It was obvious Roland had talked to them.

Mom said, "Bob, I don't like him quitting. He really loves baseball. If he runs away from what he loves, what's going to happen to Tip when he bumps into things he doesn't like?"

"You're making too much of this, Ann. Baseball's a game and nothing more. I'm going to take Tip off the team."

No, I thought, I can't let that happen. Not yet, anyway.

I rattled the door noisily to let them know I was there. Then I opened it and walked into the living room.

They stared at me.

"My God," said Dad, "what's happened to you?"

"Are you all right, Tip?" Mom asked.

I forced a grin. "Guess what? I fell into the river."

Dad was not amused. "What were you doing there?"

"Nothing."

"Tip," said Mom, "we were getting very worried about you. I even called Mr. Corunna to find out if he knew where you were."

Now I was embarrassed.

"Well . . ." I shrugged.

"And that," Dad said grimly, "was after *I* had called him. We'll talk about it as soon as you get into dry clothes. Now you go upstairs and change!"

I was in for it all right.

Roland was in his room playing his stereo. I opened his door. "Thanks a lot, pal."

"What did you say?"

"I said, 'Thanks a lot!' "

"For what?"

"Talking too much."

I slammed his door and went into the bathroom and got my wet clothes off. Roland came in after me the way little brothers do.

"I didn't tell them what you did. We were all talking about it. They overheard."

"Look, I don't want to hear about it. Just shove off, please."

"Tip, I—"

"I said I don't want to hear about it. Shove off!"

Roland stood there. "If you'd just listen to me—"

"I don't want to listen to you. All I do is listen to you. Just get out of here."

I pushed him out of the room and shut the door. I dried myself off and then got into new clothes and went downstairs.

"All right," Dad said, "what were you doing down at the river?"

"I went down there to get some peace and quiet and—" I shrugged, "I fell in."

"How does someone fifteen years old fall into a river?" Mom asked.

"It wasn't easy."

"Don't make a joke out of it," Dad said curtly. "How did it happen?"

"I saw a big carp swimming right near that old rock we fish from sometimes. I leaned over to grab it and fell in."

"Are we supposed to believe that?"

"Dad, it's true. You can smell my hands. Here, smell them."

"He does smell of fish," Mom said.

"You tried to catch a fish with your bare hands?"

"It was stupid, I admit, but he was inches away . . ."

Dad shook his head. "I don't know what's happening to you, Tip. Falling into a river. Storming home from a baseball game, interrupting Roland's rehearsal as if you owned this house . . ."

"I'm sorry about that."

"Have you told Roland you were?" Mom asked.

"No."

"I suggest you do that."

"OK, I will, Mom."

"I think we ought to find out *why* you did it," said Dad.

I knew that he knew why already. Just the way he said that. And I was right. It's Dad's way of introducing things after the fact.

"When I heard how badly you behaved with Roland, I called Mr. Corunna. I wanted to know what happened in your game."

I winced.

"And Mr. Corunna told us. Tip, things can't go on like this. You're having a hard time on the diamond, and you're taking it home and passing it on to Roland."

"I said I was sorry."

"What's going to happen the next time you let the players on the other team rattle you? Tip, I really don't think you're cut out to be a ball player. Playing ball is more than being well coordinated. It's *liking* to play ball. It's liking the atmosphere, and that includes the bench jockeying. You've got the physical equipment, Tip, but I'm not sure you've got the emotional equipment.

You're too serious about it. You can't play ball and have fun.

"Yes, I can."

"We haven't seen that yet."

"Just give me another chance. I'll figure out a way to beat this rabbit ears business."

"Tip," Dad said quietly, "would you like me to make the decision for you? Would you like to get out of baseball?"

"No."

They were silent. We all looked at one another. In the silence I could hear Roland's stereo.

"All right," Dad said finally, "you get one more chance. But if I see you coming back and messing up Roland, that's it. Now you go upstairs and apologize."

I nodded. I went upstairs. I knocked on Roland's door.

He didn't hear it. How could he?

I banged on Roland's door.

"Who is it?" he yelled.

"Me."

"What do you want now?"

I swallowed. "To apologize."

"What?"

"Turn your stereo down and you'll hear me."

He turned down his stereo. "I want to apologize." I opened his door. "I'm sorry," I said.

Roland looked at me. "No, you're not," he said.

He was only eleven years old, but he was a pretty smart kid.

"Look, I've apologized. That's it."

I went to my room. I heard him get off his bed and a second later he was in my room.

"Tip, how about joining our band?"

He had to be kidding. "I mean," he said seriously, "if you're really sorry, you could help us out by playing rhythm and singing with Peggy. We've got a real chance to win the Battle of the Bands Saturday. We've got this new kind of song; we make it up on the spot—"

"Hey, wait a second," I said. "I'm in ninth grade. There's no way I'm going to play in a band with two sixth-graders."

"Peggy's in ninth grade."

"She's a nerd."

"No, she's not. And you know it. She's a good singer and she's pretty too. Tip, we really have a chance to win Saturday. Wings and I figured out this thing. We can get the audience on our side. They join in our songs. We ask them to shout out a word like . . . *love* and then we just add *dee* and then the last part of the word. Like *lovedeedovedovedove.* And then we swing into our song: *lovedeedovedovedove, you can love it all day long. You can sing it or sway it, as long as you play it, you can make yourself a song. Songdeedongdongdong, songdeedongdongdong* . . . Get it?"

I stared at him. "That's just about the most miserable excuse for a song I've ever heard, Roland. Someone shouts a word and you add dee-deesomething. It's dumb, Roland. Real dumb."

"No, it's not. It's great. It works. We're having fun."

"Roland, I've got enough problems right now without your adding to them. Now I'd like to lie down, if it's OK with *you.*"

"*Youdeedoodoodoo,*" Roland sang desperately. "Get it?"

"I got it," I said, and shut the door in his face.

"Think about it," he shouted.

"*Nodeedododo,*" I yelled back.

"Aw, Tip," he started to go on . . .

But I turned on my radio and turned it up loud so I wouldn't hear him. There are times that noise helps.

7

Baseball Pressure, Music Pressure

It's funny how a kid brother can have the last word. And I do mean *word* too.

That night I had a hard time sleeping. Not that I was reliving the terrible ball game or my fight with Roland. It's just that I kept having crazy dreams.

In one of them, people would run up to me and shout a word. Dad, for instance, came up and shouted, "Quit" at me.

And I yelled back at him, "Quitdeeditdit-dit . . ."

And then Joe Dawkins hollered, "Chuck hard, Tip," and I shouted back at him (I wasn't even pitching in the dream), "Tipdeedipdip-dip . . ."

But it was when Peggy Anderson yelled "Rude" at me and I was shouting back at her "Rudedeedododo . . ." that I woke up.

Rudedeedododo indeed! Darn that Roland and his stupid songs.

I lay there with my eyes open. A horsefly was banging against my window screen. Trying to get out.

"Why did you come in in the first place, dummy?" I said to him.

I got up and swiped at him. And missed. I swiped again, and missed again. Three swipes and you're out, so now I concentrated. I followed him with my hand as he bounced against the screen. And then when he stopped to rest, I grabbed him.

I lifted the screen up with my free hand and let Mr. Horsefly fly off into the sunshine.

It was hot already outside. And going to be worse.

Roland was sleeping. He's a great sleeper. Most musicians are.

Our folks were gone to work. There was a note from Mom on the kitchen table.

TIP,

DON'T FORGET ABOUT MRS. KAPPLER'S BUSHES. I'LL BE HOME AT NOON FOR LUNCH.

MOM

Mom knew exactly what I needed reminding of. Mrs. Kappler's bushes were murder.

I grabbed some orange juice, Cheerios, and milk, and then went upstairs to wake up the rock star. Roland would sleep all day if I let him.

I went into his room and punched him lightly on the shoulder.

"Wake up, Roland."

He turned, opened his eyes. "Quit hitting me," he said.

"Those were love taps. It's after nine and I'm leaving."

"Where're you going?"

"Cut Mrs. Gardner's lawn and cut Mrs. Kappler's bushes. You want to help me."

"How much you paying?"

"I'll split with you."

"I'll help you with the bushes if you play in the band."

"Bargains, bargains. I'll see you later."

Roland is going to be a success because he has a one-track mind.

Mrs. Gardner lives around the block. I got her power mower out of her garage and was cutting her lawn when Joe Dawkins and Chico Morales came up on their bikes. I turned off the mower. I could hear their bikes through the mower. The greatest ears in town, I thought bitterly.

"Roland said you were working," Chico said.

"It's too hot to work," Joe said.

"It's too hot to do anything," I said.

"Yeah. Well, we got a practice today," Joe said. He and Chico looked at each other. Chico nodded. I wondered what was going on.

Joe stuck his hand in his pockets. "We brought you a present."

"What?"

"These."

He brought out two little black things.

"What're they?"

"Earplugs."

I looked at the plugs and then looked at my teammates. A wave of anger went through my body.

"I don't want'em."

"Try'em. My mother uses ones just like these when I play my records," Chico said.

"Give'em to your mother."

"Come on, Tip. Don't be so tough. Stick'em in your ear."

"Stick'em in your own ear," I said, and I turned on the mower.

Joe did just that. "Hey," he said, beaming, "I can't hear a thing."

"Can you hear the lawn mower?" Chico yelled.

"What did you say?" Joe yelled back.

Clowns. They meant well, but that's what they were. Baseball clowns. If they were trying to make me nervous about today's practice, they sure were succeeding.

I ignored them and went on cutting the lawn. After a while they went away.

It took me about a half hour to cut Mrs. Gardner's lawn and then about another hour to get away from her. She insisted on giving me milk and cookies and telling me what the neighborhood was like a hundred years ago. Finally she gave me the two bucks I got paid for cutting her lawn. That was about three bucks less than anyone else got paid, but Dad said to be quiet and take it. He'd make it up for me. Mrs. Gardner was living in the nineteenth century.

After that I went over to Mrs. Kappler's house and got her clipper out of the garage. I looked around for gloves, too, but couldn't find any. I did everything quietly. Mrs. Kappler isn't as nice as Mrs. Gardner. She hangs over you.

"Is that you, Tip?" she called out from a second-story window.

Caught. "Yes, ma'am."

"I'll be right down to show you what I want done."

It would be rotten work. Hot. Bloody too. Those barberry bushes were mean.

Mrs. Kappler came down and hovered over me while I cut and cut and got cut and cut. She kept finding more branches for me to cut. Finally she was satisfied and gave me one dollar for two hours of work.

"Now, Tip, I hope you have a bank account to put that in because a penny saved is a penny earned."

"Yes, ma'am."

"You can tell your mother you did a very good job."

I'll tell her a few more things, I thought.

Mom was making tuna fish sandwiches for me and Roland and her. Roland was in the basement, working on his songs.

"Did you—" Mom asked.

"Yes, I did." I showed her the cuts on my hands.

"All that for one dollar," I said.

She smiled. "It's a good thing to be doing, Tip, helping the older women. They live on fixed incomes."

"I live on no income."

"If we win the Battle of the Bands," Roland said, emerging from the basement, "we can make a lot of money playing at school dances in the fall."

"A pipe dream," I said. I started eating my sandwich.

"Why don't you seriously consider playing with Roland's band?" Mom asked. "It would make your summer more interesting."

"My summer's interesting enough, thanks. Mrs. Kappler has a lot more bushes for me to cut. And then I'll need time to go to the hospital to get my hands fixed. I need stitches on my left hand right now."

Mom laughed. "All right, Tip. You're having a busy summer. And that's good. What time is your baseball practice?"

"One."

"Will you want some dessert?"

"No. I better get over there right now."

8

Train Hard, Fight Easy

Dad believes in being prepared, getting ready. He's always quoting some Russian general (I think he makes these guys up) who said, "Train hard, fight easy."

Coaches believe this too. They really think that if you practice hard enough, you can do things correctly in a game situation.

It's just not true. Practice isn't real. It's knowing that something is real, for keeps, that makes you tighten up.

For example: that afternoon at the park. Mr.

Corunna was having that team practice especially for me. To work on my head. He had told me that practice was at one o'clock. But when I got there at one, everyone was already there and had been for some time. They were all warmed up. They'd been there since 12:30. He was getting them ready for me. When I arrived, they were grinning like kids in on a big secret.

Mr. Corunna didn't waste any time.

"All right, Tip, we've divided the squad into two teams . . ."

I was to pitch for the red team and Joe was to catch for both teams. Vince was going to pitch for the blues. Red and blue are the colors of our uniforms.

The blues were to bat first. Mr. Corunna would coach at third for both teams. He had a small box with him. I couldn't see what was in it. He put it down behind third base.

The leadoff man for the blues was Hilda Sims. She choked way up on the bat. Mr. Corunna had taught her to shorten her swing. As Hilda stepped in, Mr. Corunna took something out of the box. I saw it out of the corner of my eye. And then I heard it.

It was a bullhorn. A hand-held bullhorn. And he started shouting at me through it.

"Hey, hey, Tip, you're going up, up, up . . ."

I stared at him. His voice was bouncing all over the park, off the elm trees and the maples.

And that was the signal for everyone else to start hollering at me. If I thought there had been a lot of noise in the game against United Uniform, it was nothing compared to what was happening now.

We weren't the only people in the park. I saw two tennis players stop playing right in the middle of a match. A man walking a golden retriever almost fell over his dog. People pushing kids on the swings had to duck as the swings almost hit them in their frozen astonishment. And what did the people who lived in the houses on the park think? It was summer. Their windows were open.

"You stink, Tip. You're terrible. How's the rabbit ears, Tip?"

Through the din Joe came trotting out from behind the plate. He held his hand out to me.

"Change your mind?"

In his hand were the two little earplugs.

"No," I said, and I almost laughed, "I don't need them."

The whole thing was unreal. A comedy.

"Suit yourself," he said, irritated.

Willie Thomas was yelling at me in his high-pitched voice that my socks smelled, my pants were falling down, my nose was too big, and my feet were each pointing the wrong way.

I started to laugh.

Hilda Sims waved her bat at me. "Pitch it if you can, Tip," she hollered.

"Sure, Hilda," I yelled back. I wound up and fogged a strike right down the middle through the sea of noise.

"Lucky," Mr. Corunna roared through the bullhorn.

"He won't do it again," Willie yelled.

"Look at me, Tip," Mr. Corunna hollered. "Look at me."

I looked at him, winked at him, wheeled and fired another strike past Hilda.

She popped up on my third pitch.

After that I struck out Ed Tinker and Vince Mendoza on six straight fastballs.

And that shut them up.

Mr. Corunna met me as I came to the bench. He was grinning. "See, Tip, you can do it, can't you?"

He was a nice man who really thought things could work out simply.

"Tip, you're starting Thursday night against Belden." He turned to the rest of them. "I think we've done it, gang. We've shown something to Tip. We've showed him he can pitch through a lot of bench jockeying. Nobody will yell louder than I yelled at you, Tip. Good going."

Everyone congratulated me. Everyone except Joe Dawkins. He didn't look convinced. He wasn't the only one. I wasn't either. Practice is one thing, a game's another. These guys meant well. Belden Hardware wouldn't on Thursday night.

On the other hand, Belden Hardware was a really good team. And I thought they just might be above taunting and yelling at me.

9

The Game against
Belden Hardware

They weren't.

Maybe it was our team's fault because Chico got on right away on an error. And then Ed Tinker caught an inside fastball and tripled down the left-field line. And then George hit a wrong-way home run down to right field. Before Belden ever came to bat, it was 3–0 against them.

It was a long time since anyone had scored three runs against Belden, no less in the first inning.

Mr. Corunna was clapping his hands. "All

right, that's the way to start it out. Now, Tip, you hold'em. They won't see your swift one today. Fog it through there, boy.''

I took some nice, easy warm-up tosses and then fogged a few fast balls at Joe. The Beldens watched me silently. They were all big guys and good players. They came from the Sumpter Street neighborhood of Arborville. A poor section. They didn't have money to go to summer camp and things. They played ball all year round as a team: baseball, football, basketball. They were tough. I was pretty sure they wouldn't resort to the screaming bit.

Their first batter was their shortstop. He looked older than fifteen. He practically had a mustache. I wound up and fired a fastball down the middle.

He was taking all the way. Strike one.

My team cheered. I felt loose. Maybe I'd been wrong about the crazy practice.

The batter dug in. I wound up and fired just a bit low.

"That's more like it, Tip," someone hollered from their bench.

"Make him get them over, Ike," another Belden shouted.

"He can't pitch, Ike," their third base coach yelled.

I sure can, I answered silently.

I fired my third pitch chin high, but Ike went for it.

"Don't help him out, Ike," their coach yelled. "He'll walk you if you let him."

"Hey, Tip," another guy yelled, "how're the old rabbit ears today?"

"Can't hear a thing you say," I shouted back to him.

"Don't talk to him, Tip," Joe yelled. "Don't listen to him."

"He's got them rabbit ears on today," the batter on deck hollered to the bench.

And their bench hollered back . . . at me.

Nuts to you, I thought. I wound up and I guess I wanted that strike a little too hard. I held on to the ball too long. It bounced about a foot in front of the plate. Now they were all whooping it up. It was the three-run lead of ours. They were scared. They'd do anything to get back in the ball game. And they did.

They started riding me and I heard it all and lost my temper and hollered back at them. I ended up walking the leadoff batter, walking their second batter, and hitting the number three hitter.

It was like pitching in a howling wind. All I heard were people shouting at me and me shouting back at them.

Joe called time and trotted out to the mound. "OK, Tip," he said grimly, "put these in your ears."

"What's he giving him, ump?" their bench yelled.

Chico came over from shortstop.

"Stand in front of him," Joe ordered.

Chico stood between me and the Belden bench. I stuck an earplug in each ear.

Joe said something to me.

"What?" I said.

He grinned and slapped me on the back. Then he stuck his mouth close to my ear and hollered, "We'll get these bums out one-two-three."

It was odd now. Playing in silence. Cars were going by on Stadium Boulevard and they were probably honking horns, but I couldn't hear a thing. An airplane went overhead on its way to Detroit Metro, but I couldn't hear that either. And on the sidelines the Hardwares were all shouting at me—their mouths were working hard—but I couldn't hear them either.

The runners led off. The batter said something to me. What? It looked like he was saying, *You're wild, Tip. Wild.*

The third base coach waved at me and silently shouted something that looked like, *Tip, you can't pitch. You can't pitch.* At least that's what his lips seemed to be saying.

I was actually trying to lip-read their insults. Was I nuts? I guess I was. I was forgetting to get on with the ball game. Finally the ump held out his hands and came running out to the mound.

I couldn't hear what he was saying. I removed an earplug.

". . . delay of game . . ." he was saying. "Start pitching."

"Sure," I said.

The third base coach spotted what was happening.

"He's wearing earplugs," he shouted to his bench.

I put the plug back in and shut him out.

Now they were all pantomiming me, grinning, pointing to their ears, laughing, making fake rabbit ears and sticking their index fingers in them.

The ump was talking to me. I couldn't lip-read him. He was saying something like *play* or *pitch.*

I fired wide.

Their runners danced off. I didn't look at them. I couldn't hear them.

This time I fired one down the middle. The batter popped it up . . . off to my right. I ran for it. It was funny running in silence. You don't often think about it but when you run you can hear yourself run. You know how far you're off the ground from the sounds of your feet, where the bumps are in the ground, especially important when you're looking up in the air, concentrating on the ball.

I couldn't hear anyone shout. I couldn't hear anyone else trying for the ball.

But I sure felt it.

Ed Tinker and I collided. We both went flying. The ball fell between us.

One of my earplugs fell out and then I could hear the screaming and hollering.

They got two runs in before I picked up the ball.

Mr. Corunna called time and walked out slowly to the mound.

"All right, Tip," he said quietly, "you can come out now. Vince!"

He waved Vince in from left field.

"I thought the earplugs would help," Joe said lamely.

"I'm not knocking you," Mr. Corunna said, "but you can't play this game in silence. You were calling Tip off the ball and he never heard you. Tip, I don't know what to do about you. Honest to God, I don't know what to do. Try and hold them, Vince."

He gave the ball to Vince, and then he and I walked to the bench.

I got a good set of jeers from the Beldens.

"Hey, man, you're supposed to wear earplugs when you go swimming" was one I'll never forget.

Our fans were deathly silent. I was glad once again my folks weren't there. I sat down at the far end of the bench away from Mr. Corunna. I was glad when Vince finished his warm-ups and the game resumed. We had a 3–2 lead and Vince pitched his heart out protecting it.

Chico went the last two innings, and with the help of some great fielding he didn't let them get any runs. We beat the Beldens.

10
Quitting—Joining

Maybe the real problem is that I don't have the temperament to be a ball player. Dad said that, but I didn't really believe it till we rode home from Vets Park in Mr. Corunna's truck. Everyone was happy except me. I should have been happy. We'd won the game. Instead, I sat in the corner of the truck feeling rotten.

Ego, ego, ego. Always worried about how *I* do, how *I* look. It's like pushing a load of bricks down the road all the time.

The guys were kind to me. They slapped me

on the back as though I had something to do with the victory. Mr. Corunna didn't say anything to me though. He was disgusted with me. And rightly so.

He took us to the parking lot at Sampson Park. Most everyone lived near the park.

"Good game, Joe."

"Good game, Willie."

"Way to go, Bobby . . ."

"See you, Hilda . . ."

One by one they jumped out, shouting.

I climbed down and started out of the lot. No one called "good game" to me or "later . . ." Maybe they were hoping they wouldn't see me later.

It was time to get out. Time to quit. It would be in the best interest of everyone. No matter how much you love something, there comes a time when your love could be hurting the people around you.

People get down on quitters. But sometimes it takes more guts to quit than it does to stay. Especially when you want to stay.

I wondered how my folks would take it. Especially my mom.

She was outside, gardening in the fading light.

She has a rose bush she's very proud of. Mom loves gardening. She says you forget about your troubles gardening. That's the sport for me, I thought. Chasing weeds, scooping them up, and firing them into the trash barrel. People don't yell at gardeners. Hey gardener, gardener. Flowers don't yell. Weeds go quietly. Between fishing and gardening, I could have a good summer.

I walked into our yard. "Hello, Tip," Mom said, looking up, "how did it go?"

"We won. What are those flowers?"

"Tip, you mean you beat Belden Hardware?"

"Yeah. The blues there."

"They're campanula. But Tip, that's marvelous. And you pitched."

"I didn't get through the first inning. Vince and Chico won it for us."

"Oh, Tip," Mom said.

"It's no problem. I'm going to quit. Dad's right. I'm not a ball player. I don't have the head to be a competitor. I've got rabbit ears. I'll always have them. I'm quitting the team."

"I'm sorry to hear that."

"Mom, please don't make a speech about how important it is not to quit. There are times when you just have to do what you think is right. This baseball thing is no good for me; it's no good for the team."

Mom was silent.

"What are those flowers called?" I asked.

"Which ones?"

"The funny red ones."

"Bergamot."

"How can you know the names of all the flowers?"

"How can you know the names of major league baseball players? You know about what you like."

"Do you think I could like flowers the way you do?"

She laughed. "I don't know."

"I'd like to. I'm going to have to do something instead of baseball."

I'd given her an opening. I hadn't meant to.

"How about helping Roland with his band."

"Oh, Mom."

"Think about it, Tip. It would make Roland happy. It would make us happy. It'd be something you're good at. Your ears would be helpful there. If you played with Roland's band, I might at least see some good out of your quitting your team."

"I don't want to do it, though."

"Why not? You're a fine musician."

"It's not that. It's just—"

"That it's your little brother's band."

I hesitated. And then I nodded. She'd hit the mark.

"Tip, one sign of growing up is forgetting about yourself. And doing the right thing just because it's the right thing to do. You're getting in your own way, Tip."

She wasn't telling me anything more than I'd told myself in Mr. Corunna's truck.

"Think about it, Tip."

"I will."

Just then I heard our Aspen coming down the lane. It had squeaky brakes. You always heard it coming.

I watched Dad back it into the driveway. And then he and Roland got out.

"Go help them unload," Mom said.

"Right."

Dad looked up from the tailgate. "Tip. How'd the game go?"

"We won."

"Wonderful! You beat the Beldens."

"Yep."

"Did you pitch?"

I hesitated. Grinned. "For a while."

Roland came around the station wagon. "You really beat'em, Tip?"

"Sure did."

He held out his palm and we slapped hands.

"I'll carry the amp with you," I said.

"I'll get the rest of the gear," Dad said.

Roland and I took the amp through the garage and then to the back door.

"It's great you beat those guys. They won the championship last year, didn't they?"

"Yeah. Watch the door now."

"I see it. How many innings did you pitch?"

"I didn't get anyone out. Vince saved the day. OK, going down."

"I'm sorry, Tip."

"It's not your fault, kid. Almost down . . ."

"It's not your fault either that you hear too much, Tip. All musicians do. That's why I worked out our new song. I wanted to use our musician's ears."

"Roland, forget it. It's a dumb song."

We set his amplifier down gently.

"No, it's not," Roland insisted. "It's going to make us different from the other bands."

"What's the name of your band anyway?" I was only trying to change the subject from his

Songdeedongdongdong song.

"The Aces."

"Three Aces?"

"I know. That's what everyone says. We need a fourth ace if we want to win."

"When's the big battle?"

"Saturday." Roland looked at me. "Are you changing your mind, Tip?"

"Maybe."

His face lighted up. "Oh, Tip, that'd be great. Paul and Peggy are coming over tonight. We can work tonight and tomorrow. You'll fit right in. The songs aren't hard. You'll pick them up right away. And *Songdeedongdongdong* is a snap—"

"No chance of dropping that number, is there?"

"Aw, Tip . . ." And then *Roland* changed the subject. "And your guitar's in great shape too."

"How do *you* know?"

He looked embarrassed. "I been playing it from time to time."

I laughed. "I bet you have. OK, Roland. But just for Saturday. No more after that."

"Fair enough!" Roland was happy. He ran up the stairs.

"Where're you going?"

"Call Paul and Peggy and tell them the news. Also I want them over earlier. We've got a lot of work to do."

He got on the phone. I sat down and looked at his amplifier. Well, at least I was making someone happy. That was an improvement.

Before we started rehearsing, I talked everything over with Mom and Dad. They were caught between feeling sad that I'd quit ball and happy that I was making music with Roland.

"Why does it have to be an either–or?" Dad asked.

"Because it is," I said.

"Well, you better call Mr. Corunna."

"Maybe I can wait on that."

"Tip," Mom warned.

I dreaded doing this. But I had to do it. I went upstairs to the phone in their bedroom. I didn't want anyone listening in on this. I took a deep breath. And I called Mr. Corunna.

"What's up, Tip?" he asked.

"I . . . uh . . . Mr. Corunna. I'm quitting baseball."

Silence.

"Say that again, Tip," he said. His voice sounded grim. Why on earth would he want to keep me on the team? He ought to be doing a dance.

I swallowed. "I'm quitting baseball."

"I don't get it," he said. "We win a big one over Belden Hardware and you want to quit."

"I didn't help you win it, Mr. Corunna. I almost lost it for you."

"Tip, you can help us at other positions. You can hit. You can throw."

"They'll ride me when I come to bat. I guess I've got those old rabbit ears, Mr. Corunna. And they're no good for baseball. I'll bring my uniform over to you tomorrow."

"Tip, we'll talk about it after the game against United Uniform on Monday. We're playing on Diamond Four at Buhr. I'll see you there at five o'clock."

And then he hung up on me.

"I'm not sure this is a free country," I said to Mom and Dad. "I was just upstairs calling Mr. Corunna. I told him I quit, and he won't let me."

They tried not to look pleased. "Maybe you've got a civil liberties case, Tip."

"No. I'm just not going to show up at Monday's game. Then he'll know I'm serious."

Mom and Dad said nothing. They had said all they were going to say on the subject of me and baseball.

Peggy Anderson and Paul Wings came over our house around nine o'clock. They looked a little doubtfully at me.

"What made you change your mind?" Peggy asked.

"I just feel like it."

"Don't do us any favors," she said.

"I'm not."

"Roland's lead guitar," Wings reminded me.

"I know that. Roland's a better musician than I am."

That took a little of the chill off.

"But I can play a little. And sing."

"Can you?" Peggy said.

"Tip's got a swell voice," Roland said nervously. "Let's start with . . ." he didn't dare look at me ". . . a *songdeedongdongdong.*"

"OK?" Peggy asked, challenging me.

"Kaydeekaykaykay," I replied.

She laughed. And we swung into it.

II

Battle of the Bands

Saturday afternoon we played music in Sampson Park—the same park we practice baseball in. I kept praying the two wouldn't get mixed up. That none of my teammates would come around. I don't think any of them liked music, but you never know; when bands get going real loud, a lot of different kinds of people come flocking.

At first, though, I wasn't sure there'd be anyone there at all. A Battle of the Bands is, I think, a pretty silly idea. Kind of juvenile. A music war. When we got there, though, there were already about fifty kids sitting in the grass watching everyone set up.

There were five bands in all: a tenth-grade band, a ninth-grade band, an eighth-grade band, a seventh-grade band, and ours—the Aces—a mixed band.

Roland slapped hands with the other musicians and, to my embarrassment, introduced me around.

"This is my brother, Tip. Tip, this is Charley Hauck from Pioneer."

Pioneer is one of Arborville's two high schools. It blew my mind that my little brother knew high school students.

"Didn't know you had a brother, O'Hara," Hauck said. And he nodded at me. I was now known as Roland O'Hara's brother!

The Arborville Recreation Department had set up generators, and we began plugging our instruments into them. This ought to wake up the whole neighborhood, I thought. It would make Coach Corunna's bullhorn sound like a stage whisper. The music ought to blast the park apart.

And it did.

Starting at two o'clock, a man from the recreation department got up and introduced all the bands. The crowd of fifty had more than doubled. And more people were coming. I scanned the faces to see if any of the Acme Lumbers were there. I couldn't spot anyone. I was relieved.

We drew the order of playing by straws. The eighth-grade band went first, then the seventh, then us, then the tenth, and then the ninth.

I thought the eighth-grade band was pretty good. They imitated a whole variety of rock bands and played some dancy tunes. What they didn't have was a personality of their own. I began to see the sense of Roland's *Songdeedongdongdong.*

The seventh-grade band was pretty bad. But everyone kindly clapped for them.

And then we were up: two sixth-graders and two ninth-graders.

Roland's plan was to "hit them with who we are right away."

So the kid—and I got to hand it to him, he was scared but brave—went up to the microphone and said:

"We're the Aces. The Four Aces."

Laughter. As though you could have a deck with only three aces.

"And we've got a new kind of song. We need your help to make it work. We want you to give us some of the lyrics. Like if you shout out a word—any word—we'll stick it in our song."

"Like 'rock'?" a girl called out.

"Rock it is," Roland called back to her. He turned to us. "Rock," he yelled.

And we sang back to him, and them:

Rockdeedockdockdock
Rockdeedockdockdock
You can rock it all day long
You can sing it or sway it
As long as you play it
You can make yourself a song
Songdeedongdongdong
Songdeedongdongdong

People started to laugh. Another girl called out, "Kiss."

"Kiss," Roland hollered at us.

Kissdeedissdissdiss
Kissdeedissdissdiss
You can kiss it all day long (laughter from the
    audience!)
You can sing it or sway it
As long as you play it
You can make yourself a song

Songdeedongdongdong
Songdeedongdongdong

And then suddenly lots of people were shouting words at us. Words like: "Baby!"

And we did a *babydeedeedee, babydeedeedee, you can baby it all day long.* . . that had them laughing, and got the old park rocking.

Someone called out, "Love . . ."

And, of course, we knew that one.

And a grown-up man shouted, "Kids."

And we swung into *kidsydididid, kidsydididid, you can kid it all day long* . . .

And a boy yelled out, "Katydid."

And, laughing ourselves, we sang back to them, *katydiddiddid* . . .

And another kid yelled, "Katy did what?"

And we handed back to him, *whatdeedutdutdut.*

Everyone was clapping and cheering and laughing and trying to get their words into our song.

They wouldn't let us get on to our other songs—our straight songs—but we did, and when we thought we were finished with our set, they made us sing another *songdeedongdongdong.* And this time the word was "Sampson Park . . ."

So we did a *Sampson Parkdeedarkdarkdark* that

82

got them all singing with us. We'd turned the battle of the bands into a gigantic singalongdee-dongdongdong.

That old park was really shaking. People came out of their houses and sat down on the front steps and watched.

Yet, even as we played, I couldn't help noticing that life went on in the park as usual. People went on playing tennis; there were college kids hooping on the basketball court, and a Saturday softball game was going on at Diamond Two.

And the usual dogs running around in circles, baby carriages, and little kids watching the Battle of the Bands from their fathers' shoulders.

Finally the audience let us go. And the tenth-grade band played. They were smooth and polished. The ninth-grade band wasn't very good. I figured it had to be between us and the tenth-graders.

The judges were three music teachers from the school system. One of them handed a slip of paper to the man from the recreation department.

He picked up the mike. My heart began to pound. Suddenly this was important too. As important as baseball. Maybe even more important.

The man said, "In the opinion of the judges,

the winner of this Battle of the Bands is . . ." He paused, looked up, and said, "The Aces!"

Cheers went up.

"Peggy Anderson, Roland O'Hara, Tip O'Hara, and Paul Wings. The Aces!"

People were clapping. Roland and Paul were jumping up and down, slapping palms like ball players.

I just sat there and laughed. It was nice to be a winner for once. And feel like I'd helped us win. And odd that, of all people, my kid brother had made it possible.

After that we signed autographs for little kids and talked to other musicians. They came over and shook our hands.

"Congrats, Roland. You guys sounded fine-deedinedinedine."

Roland giggled. "You guys were great too."

It was almost like baseball. With this difference. In baseball, the winners came over to shake hands with the losers. This was the other way around. And it wasn't like they were losers. They had made fine music too, and everyone had enjoyed themselves.

Peggy Anderson kissed Roland. She kissed Wings. Then she came over to me and stuck out her hand. "We wouldn't have won it without your help, Tip."

"Hey," I said, "don't I get a kiss too?"

She blushed. And then I guess I blushed too. Our two little sixth-grade musicians yelled together:

"Kiss him too, Peggy. He's in the band."

So, blushing, she kissed me.

At which point Roland took over again. He couldn't stop talking. He had lots of plans for the fall. There were going to be lots of school dances we could play at. Make money too. He and Wings were going to write more songs.

This wasn't the time to remind Roland that I was only in this for today. That one gig, even a winning one, doesn't make a career. That I still had other things to do. But Roland was so happy and excited that all I said was that we had best get our gear out of the park before it got ripped off.

Kids were all over our instruments, poking fingers at the knobs on our amps. Wings's father had a van in the parking lot, and we took turns lugging the stuff over to it. Then we all shook hands and solemnly agreed to have a band meeting early next week to talk about our future.

"We've got a real future, Tip," Roland said, as he and I walked home. "We fit together real well. Not many bands have that."

I smiled. Roland was like a puppy. "Right," I said. "But I've got lots of other things to do in the fall, Roland. I'm playing ninth-grade football and after that there's basketball, hockey . . ."

"Music'll help your sports, Tip."

I looked at him, amused. He thought he could conquer all now. "Will it? How?"

"I don't know how, but it will." Roland had that stubborn expression on his face. After all, he was a kid who got things done. Formed a rock band. Won a big contest.

"Well, Roland, the day music helps me play ball will be the day I join your band permanently."

"Do you mean that?"

"Yep."

"Good," Roland said. "I'm going to figure out a way for you to get rid of your rabbit ears."

"My rabbit ears are no problem anymore, Roland. I've quit the team."

"Maybe. But it hasn't quit on you."

"What do you mean?"

"Look."

I looked where he was looking. The front steps of our house. Practically all the Acme Lumbers were standing or sitting around there, waiting for me: George, Chico, Joe, Ed, Bobby, Willie, Hilda, Duvall . . . Their bikes were all over the lawn.

Now I was in for it.

12

Emergency Meeting

"Where you been, Tip?" Chico asked.

"Over at the park," I said.

"There's nothing there but music," George grumbled.

Roland laughed. "I was making some of it," I said. "I was playing with Roland's band."

"You're kidding," Joe said.

"No. We won the Battle of the Bands."

"Serious?" Chico asked.

"Yeah. I'm shifting gears. I guess you guys got the word. I'm giving up baseball."

"No, you're not," George said.

"That's why we're here, man," said Ed. "You can't do it."

"Look. I'm just messing up the team. You don't need me. Monday Regan's back."

"Yeah, he's back all right," Joe said, "with a busted shoulder. The jerk hurt himself on a diving board up north."

"Oh, no."

"He's out for the summer," Chico said.

"Tip," Vince said quietly, "I can't do it alone. You've got to give it another shot. You're a pitcher."

I shook my head. "I'm sorry, you guys. I'm sorry about Regan. I'm sorry about myself. I'm sorry about you. There's nothing I'd like to do better than pitch for you guys. But you saw what happened Thursday night, and the game before. It won't work."

"What are we going to do for another pitcher?" Chico asked.

"How about Bell?"

Bobby Bell shook his head. "I get the ball over, but that's it."

"He's strictly batting practice. They'll kill him."

"What about you, Ed? You got a good arm."
Tinker had a rifle arm at third.

He grinned, remembering something. "Back in the nine-year-old league, my coach tried me pitching. I threw sixteen straight balls in one game."

"You're kidding," Chico said.

"No, he ain't," Willie said. "I was there."

"That must've been some ump calling sixteen straight balls," Hilda said, awed.

"He'd of been blind if he hadn't."

"Was the seventeenth pitch a strike?" Vince asked. Only a pitcher would have asked that.

Ed shook his head. "Home run," he said.

We all laughed. It was a serious meeting, an emergency meeting, but sometimes when things are so desperate, there isn't anything you can do but laugh.

"How about Hilda?"

Hilda looked embarrassed. "I'd get rattled worse'n you, Tip."

"Look, Tipper," Joe said, "when you're on, you're one of the toughest pitchers in the league. You throw harder than Vince. You're a pitcher everywhere except between your ears. All you got to do is not listen."

"Right," I said. "And all I got to do to be a great pole vaulter is jump twenty feet. No way, you guys. I'm finished. I've quit. It's going to be music for me."

"I don't believe this," Chico said.

"You better, cause it's the truth."

They looked upset, angry. Everyone except Roland. He kept looking from me to the guys and back again. He was thinking of something. I didn't know what.

"You comin' to the United Uniform game at least?" Chico asked.

"What's the use?"

"Tip, you're stupid," Joe said angrily. He got on his bike and left. The others got on their bikes. They felt sorry for me, and they were angry at me at the same time.

When they were gone, Roland said, "Tip, I bet you can lick it."

"Let's go inside and tell Mom and Dad about the band thing."

"Wait a second," he said. "What're some of the things they shout at you?"

"Roland . . ."

"Just tell me, Tip."

I breathed out. Here we go again. "Pitcher's

going up, up, up. Pitcher, your socks smell. Hey, Tip. Hey, rabbit ears. Tip is wild. Tip is up. Anything they can think of. It doesn't make any difference what they shout, as long as I hear it and let it get to me."

"What happens when it gets to you?"

"I clutch. Tighten up."

Roland nodded. "That's cause you're taking it too seriously."

"I know that."

"They're just playing games with you."

"I know that too, for Pete's sake. I'm not stupid."

"Well, then, how about playing games back with them? How about making the serious business funny?"

Those words had a familiar ring to them. *Fishin's a serious business*—down at the river, the two fishermen when I fell into the river and started laughing.

"All right, Roland, what's on your mind?"

Roland told me what was on his mind.

"That's cockeyed," I said.

"It could work."

"Not on the diamond."

"What do you have to lose?"

"I could have another rotten time."

"You could also have a great time."

"Look, Roland, I told everyone I quit."

"You can change your mind. They want you to. They need you."

It was really funny. My kid brother . . . trying to help me. It embarrassed me a little. I gave him a light punch on the shoulder.

Roland blushed. "We need you in the band, Tip. You said before if music helped you with sports, you'd play regularly with us."

I'd said that OK. It was just like Roland to put two things together that didn't go together.

"All right," I said, "but if this doesn't work . . . If I make a fool of myself again, I'll never go near your band. How about that?"

Now it was Roland's turn to hesitate. His chin quivered and then it got grim. "Fair enough," he said. "It's a good idea."

"It's a crazy idea, but I'll try it. For you."

We went inside to tell our folks about the big band victory.

They were tickled pink. It made them happy that Roland and I were winners together. Brothers usually scrap a lot, and we're no exception. So when it worked out that we won something together, it was really a plus for the family.

My folks were also happy when I told them I was going to give baseball one more try.

Roland looked questioningly at me. I shook my head. No, I wasn't going to tell our folks what our game plan was. It was pretty silly on the surface. So I laid the whole thing on Regan's injury.

"They need me. So I'll give it one last shot."

"You better call Mr. Corunna," Mom said.

"Right."

This call was even harder to make than the other one. The other call was to tell him I was quitting. This call was telling him I was someone who couldn't make up his mind. No wonder I fell apart under pressure.

"It's Tip O'Hara, Mr. Corunna."

"Yes, Tip."

Here goes nothing, I thought.

"I wonder if I could change my mind and stay with the team?"

There was a brief silence, and then Mr. Corunna made it easy for me.

"You heard about Regan, did you?"

"Yes, sir."

"I appreciate your loyalty, Tip. I'm going to

start Vince. But by league rules he can only go two innings because he pitched seven the last time out. So it's you or Chico or anyone who can get the ball over the plate."

"I'd like to try pitching one more time, Mr. Corunna."

"That's the spirit, Tip. You can do it. You've got a great arm. All you've got to do is *not* listen."

That was only the fortieth time he'd told me that. For a second I was tempted to tell him that I was only trying to pitch because of Roland's plan. And if I followed Roland's plan to a tee, it meant, in a way, listening *twice as hard*.

I decided not to. He might think I was nuts. Which I probably was.

"Monday night. Eight o'clock. Under the lights at Vets Park."

"I'll be there."

13
Tipdeedipdipdip

Vets Park under the lights. It's where the action is in Arborville on hot summer nights. Four softball diamonds and one baseball diamond. Lots of spectators. Not just folks and friends, but people out to see some excitement. Sometimes they wander from one game to another. There's a feeling of tension in the air.

The game was scheduled to start at eight. I got down there early with my family. I could see five Acme Lumbers warming up on the sidelines. George, Joe, Duvall, Hilda, Ed. They were glad to see me.

Joe fetched another ball so he and I could play catch.

He grinned. "I thought you'd make your comeback, Tip."

I laughed. My arm felt good. Loose. But then it always felt loose before a game started.

On the other side of the diamond, a half-dozen United Uniform kids were warming up. I heard them talking.

"O'Hara's there."

"Let's hope they pitch him."

"They got to. Mendoza went seven against the Hardwares."

Joe looked at me to see if I'd heard. I winked at him. He shook his head, thinking that I was listening too much already. He blistered a ball at me. I caught it, jerking my hand back to take the sting off it. Then I fired a smoker right back at him.

"Hey, take it easy," he yelled. "Save it for the game."

Mr. Corunna's truck rattled into the parking area and the rest of the team piled out. They ran toward us. Mr. Corunna liked to have everyone move fast, even if you were only going for a drink of water.

"Looking good, Tip."

"Nice to have you back, man."

It was the shortest retirement in history.

Roland, Mom, and Dad were sitting about six rows up in the stands behind third. Roland's eyes and mine met. He was reminding me of something. I nodded. I wouldn't forget.

Vince and I warmed up with Joe and Duvall. Since our team was the home team, we took the field first for infield practice. Mr. Corunna slapped the ball around. The guys looked sharp under the lights. It was exciting playing before a crowd. I didn't even mind the little pit of nervousness in my stomach. You had to feel a little nervous to be sharp.

When United Uniform took the field, Mr. Corunna seated us on the bench.

"All right," he said, "no big speeches. This is the team we've been waiting to get back at. They had no right to beat us last week. We beat the Beldens, we should murder these guys. They can't hit; they've got no pitching. Let's jump'em right away. Vince is starting. He'll go two.

Then—" he paused, and his mouth got grim—
"Tip is coming in. And when Tip comes in, I
want you guys to shout like you've never shouted
before for him."

"Coach," I said, "is it OK if they don't shout.
I think I may have a way to lick my rabbit ears.
But . . ." here goes nothing, I thought; he might
send me packing right now ". . . but I've got
to hear what they're saying."

That did it. Mr. Corunna looked at me as
though I'd escaped from a loony bin. "What did
you just say, Tip?"

I could feel my teammates stirring on the
bench, looking at me curiously.

I repeated that I wanted to listen closely to
what the United Uniform team was calling me.

"Tip," Mr. Corunna said sadly, "that won't
do at all. I'm afraid that I'll have to pitch Chico."

"Let me give it a try, Coach. One more
chance."

He hesitated. I'd never begged for a chance
to pitch before.

George said, "What've we got to lose?"

"Let him try it, Coach," Joe said.

Mr. Corunna looked doubtful. Then he
shrugged. "All right. We'll give it a try. You

99

heard what Tip wants, men. No one talking it up for him."

He kept shaking his head, and then he went on to read the batting order as though there, at least, he could find some sense. By that time United Uniform had finished their infield practice.

Mr. Corunna and Joe gave our lineup to the ump and to their coach and captain, and then we took the field.

Vince looked tall and fast out on the mound. You always look faster under the lights. Vince didn't waste many pitches. He was always around the plate. They're not really good hitters, except with their mouths. They were swinging behind the ball.

They went down one, two, three.

In the bottom half of the first we got a couple of hits but couldn't score.

In the top of the second Vince struck out the side. But as they went out to their positions, they were grinning. They were thinking: that's all for Mendoza. Now we get Tip O'Hara and his rabbit ears.

Once more I looked toward the stands. Roland was looking at me. We grinned at each other.

"Warm up, Tip," Mr. Corunna said to me.

The United Uniform bench clapped when they saw me warming up.

"Don't pay them no attention," Eddie Duvall said to me as I threw to him.

On the contrary, I thought . . .

United Uniform had just made their first mistake. Cheering the sight of me. It got our guys pepped up.

Ed Tinker, looking mean, stepped into the first pitch from the United Uniform pitcher and hit a double down the left field line. Then Vince laced a ground ball off their pitcher's shins. Ed stopped at third. Willie, who probably had the prettiest swing on our team, brought them both home with a line drive that got between the left and center fielder and rolled all the way to the fence. Willie was held up at third by Mr. Corunna.

But on the very next pitch, he stole home on a rattled United Uniform pitcher.

We had three runs before anyone was out. They changed pitchers and the new guy got the side out. But it was 3–0 when I went in. A nice cushion.

The guys made little fists at me, touched me, but said nothing.

Not the United Uniforms, though. A chorus

of cheers and jeers greeted me as I came to the mound for my warm-up tosses.

"If it isn't our old pal, Tip O'Hara."

"How're those shoelaces, Tip?"

Reminding me of the balk in the last game between us.

I winked at Joe and threw easily to him. He whipped the balls back to me. I glanced at Roland. He nodded to me. I nodded back.

Finally I had the last of my warm-up pitches. Joe fired down to second. The guys whipped the ball around with a lovely rhythm, and Ed Tinker brought it over to the mound. Joe came out too.

"OK, Tip, you fire that fast one, man. They can't see a thing tonight."

Joe looked at me gravely. "Pitch deaf, Tip," he said. "Pitch deaf."

I almost laughed. I didn't.

"Let's go, Acme," the ump called. "Batter up."

The first United Uniform hitter stepped in. As Joe squatted to give me a signal—one for fast and two for off-speed—the shouting began in earnest.

"Look here, Tip."

"How's the rabbit ears, Tip?"

Their adult coaches were both hollering at me (against the rules), "You can't pitch, Tip. Tip, you're no good."

My heart began to pound. I could feel my muscles tightening. Come on, O'Hara, I thought, you've got Roland's game plan: use it!

But they were shouting so many different words at me, it was a blur of sound.

And then, bless his heart, their third base coach—a fat man—bellowed louder than everyone: "Tip! Tip! Tip!"

I heard that "Tip" all right. I took a deep breath and repeated it inside my head. "Tipdeedipdipdip . . ." and I grinned. It had a nice ring to it. *Tipdeedipdipdip. You could Tip it all day long. You can sing it or sway it, as long as you play it. You can make yourself a song . . .*

I felt my muscles relax.

I pumped, kicked, and fired a strike right across the heart of the plate.

"Lucky!" their bench screamed at me.

"Luckdeeduckduckduck," I thought, grinning. I was loose. I pumped, kicked, and fired a fast ball right over the kid's knees for strike two. He was taking all the way. They'd all be taking. They were waiting for my rabbit ears to destroy me.

They were waiting for me to blow my cool. They were waiting, waiting, waiting . . .

And went on shouting, shouting, shouting . . .

"Tip, you stink!"

Stinkydinkdinkdink (what else?) for strike three!

"Tip, your laces are untied!"

Tidydiediedied I sang to myself and fired fast balls right down the middle.

O *songdeedongdongdong,* I love you!

They filled the air with insults. They screamed, they jeered, they hollered, they shouted.

It was music to my ears.

14

"Don't Lose'em, Just Use'em"

We beat United Uniform 8–0. But I've got to hand it to those guys. They never quit yelling. At the end of the game, they weren't just losers, they were hoarse losers.

We went over to shake hands with them. They hardly touched our hands. And they wouldn't look at us.

Our guys were grinning. The only one who said anything was Hilda. She couldn't hold it back.

"You boys got mighty pretty voices," she said.
Then we burst out laughing.

Their coach shook hands with me. "Nice game, Tip," he said. "We couldn't get to you this time."

Nor next, nor the time after next . . . nor anytime, I thought.

I said, "Thanks."

Back at our bench, the team let it all out. Whooping and jumping and slapping palms. It was a bigger victory than the one over Belden because it meant we had another starting pitcher again. Mr. Corunna was pumping my dad's hand.

"I don't know what you did for the boy, Mr. O'Hara."

"Didn't do a thing," Dad said. "I don't know what was going on either."

"It was Roland," I said. "It was his plan."

They all looked at Roland. My kid brother was grinning from ear to ear.

"Tip's going to play in my band regularly now," he said.

Joe Dawkins looked questioningly at me.

"That's right," I said. "I promised Roland if

he figured out a way for me to lose my rabbit ears, I'd play in his band. I'm not giving up baseball, though. They can go together. Music and ball. In fact, that's how I lost my rabbit ears."

Roland, who had been helping Eddie Duvall stuff the equipment bag, stopped right in the middle of helping and began to beat out a rhythm on the bag.

"Don't lose'em, just use'em," he chanted. "Rabbit ears, rabbit ears."

He was making up another song already.

"Hey, Roland," I said, "we better explain."

"OK," Roland said. He took a deep breath and then shouted, "Tip's wild. Wild."

Grinning, I said, "Wildeedilddilddild . . ."

And then Roland and I sang together:

Wildeedildilddild
Wildeedilddilddild
You can wild it all day long
You can sing it or sway it
As long as you play it
You can make yourself a song
Songdeedongdongdong
Songdeedongdongdong

The guys just stared at us as though we'd gone off our rockers.

"Get another word, Roland," I said.

Roland stuck out his belly, imitating United Uniform's fat third base coach. "Tip! Tip! Tip!" he shouted in a fake deep voice.

"Tipdeedipdipdip," I said softly, and now as I said it I went through my pitching motion.

And still they didn't get it.

"Tip is up, up, up," Roland chanted.

"Updeedupdupdup," I said, and pumped, kicked, and fired an imaginary baseball.

And, finally, they got it.

"Man, I see what you're doing," Willie said. "You're taking their bad words and funnin' 'em."

"That's right." And then I confessed all, and explained that it was Roland's idea that thinking *songdeedongdongdong* on the mound the way we'd been singing it with the band might just relax me.

"And it did," I said, grinning.

Chico said, "Tip stinks."

"Stinkydinksdinksdinks," I said.

"Hey pitcher," Hilda yelled, "your socks smell."

"Smelldeedelldelldell," I said. And added: "You can smell it all day long . . ."

They laughed. And then the cat was out of the bag and they were shouting things like, *Hellodeedododo* and good *gamedeedamedamedame*.

Meanwhile Roland sat down and started pounding the equipment bag again. "If you got'em, don't blot'em, rabbit ears, rabbit ears . . ."

Mr. Corunna just shook his head. "I never heard of anything like this in my life," he said. "But it worked. Tip, you were cool out there."

"Don't you mean cooldeedooldooldool, Coach?" Hilda asked solemnly.

That broke everyone up and got them trying still more words. The Acme Lumbers were as loose and together as we'd ever been. It was going to be a happy season again.

Driving home, Mom and Dad were happy.

"When brothers stick together," said Dad, "there's no telling what good things can happen."

"You boys ought to write a song about this," Mom said.

"I've got it started already," Roland said.

And he sang out:

Don't lose'em, just use'em
Rabbit ears, rabbit ears
You got'em, don't blot'em
Rabbit ears, rabbit ears

We drove home with Roland making up verses all the way about my old rabbit ears. It was fun listening.